This book is dedicated to Mary Retzlaff

THE PICKLE-CHIFFON PIE OLYMPICS

by

Jolly Roger Bradfield

Purple House Press
KENTUCKY

Her Royal Highness, Princess Sierra, was returning home after graduating from Princess College.

Her older sister had recently left on her honeymoon after graduating from the same school. Sierra and her sister were very much alike — except Sierra had flaming red hair and what her mother called an 'independent streak.'

Her father, the king, was more direct...he said she had 'the stubbornness of two mules.'

The king had been practicing his golf in front of the castle when she dashed up in her carriage — horses snorting and trumpeters loudly announcing her arrival.

He was so startled by the sudden racket he hit a ball right through a priceless, centuries-old stained glass window.

"Drat!" he muttered. "The queen isn't going to like that!" With a sigh he called, "Guard! Call the queen! Princess Sierra is home!" He hoped that the queen wouldn't notice the window in all the excitement.

The queen was in the kitchen, supervising the baking of a large number of Pickle-Chiffon Pies. She did this every single day, as she was the only one in the kingdom who knew how to make them exactly right — and the king demanded they be made to perfection. They were his favorite dessert in the whole world.

When the guard called, she dropped everything (including a large bowl of pickles) and raced out of the kitchen, knocking over a table, a chair, and two assistant chefs.

"My baby! My baby!" she cried. "She's *home!*" Now, Princess Sierra had just graduated from college so she certainly wasn't a baby...but that's the way mothers talk. Even queen mothers.

It was a joyous reunion, with hugs and laughter and kisses.

Immediately after unpacking, the princess told them of her plans. As her sister had just done, she wanted to get married.

"Of course my dear," said the king. "But let's not rush into things. You just got home. We'll talk about it later."

"We'll talk about it right *now!*" replied Princess Sierra stubbornly. "I've made up my mind, and I've even decided whom I wish to wed...Prince Charminger!"

"CHARMINGER? That...that..." cried the king. "Never! I forbid it!"

"But he's so *cute*, Daddy. He's got curly hair and dimples!"

"Curly hair and dimples are not reasons to get married, child!" And that was that.

(At least for a while.)

As soon as they heard of Princess Sierra's return, every royal bachelor for miles around flocked to the castle. All were attracted by her rare beauty, her curly red hair and her charming ways.

(And her Pickle-Chiffon Pie)

King Roger
the Jolly

Prince Rupert
the Rascal

Palladino
the Paunchy

Gaylord
Grapplehook

Prince

King
Bruno the Bald

Prince Leonardo
Cuddlypuss

Sir Percy
Peasoup

Prince
Musselbaum

Sir Desmond
Dimwit

Henry the
VIII, IX and X

Prince Romeo
Porkpinus

Ivan the
Tolerable

His
Honor

Sir Jack
the Rapper

Prince Welfred

Prince
Charminger

Richard the
Lionheart

Prince

Every evening she would invite them *all* to dinner (a tradition started by her recently-married sister). She always saved a seat next to her for Prince Charminger.

He was not the richest nor the brightest nobleman in the kingdom, but he was big and strong...and of course there was all that curly hair and those dimples.

he highlight of each dinner was dessert: Pickle-Chiffon Pie. But if there were too many guests — as there often were — there wouldn't be enough to go around.

Sometimes the pie had to be cut into such tiny portions that the king could hardly control his temper.

Same old story! Just like when her sister was being courted! Good grief!

"Well," said the queen, "if you'd let her get married there wouldn't be any more suitors and there would be plenty of pie to go around."

"Marry that fellow, what's his name?... Charminger? She can do much better than that. Curly hair! Dimples! Bah! That's no way to choose a husband!"

I know!" said the king finally. "I'll award the hand of the princess to the winner of the Pickle-Chiffon Pie Olympics! It's coming up soon, and that way she'll get a *real* man!"

The queen fainted.

Princess Sierra thought that was a *horrible* idea. After all, she had already chosen who she wanted to marry. "That's *awful*, Papa!" she cried. "I won't do it!

"I WON'T! I WON'T! I WON'T!"

For days there were arguments and shouts echoing through the halls of the castle.

Princess Sierra cried and stamped her foot, but to no avail. "I'll not even watch your stupid olympics! I'll go off somewhere 'til it's over! I'll go stay with Aunt Venetia!"

But the king's mind was made up. He sent out a royal decree announcing that whoever won the olympics that year would also win the hand of the princess.

And that was that.

The very next day Princess Sierra stormed out of the castle with her ladies-in-waiting and enough baggage to fill several carriages. She didn't even kiss her father goodbye.

hat night the king and queen sat in their bed sharing a whole Pickle-Chiffon Pie.

"Maybe I spoke too fast," said the king. "Maybe I should have let her marry that fellow with the dimples...Prince Charminger."

"Well, dear," said the queen, "you did what you thought best at the time. I'm sure everything will turn out fine."

But she was not *really* sure.

ignup day for the olympics was utter confusion! There were dukes and princes, rich men and poor. All wanted to marry the beautiful princess.

Some of the entrants were familiar to the royal family and some were not. They were all shapes and sizes, and all pushing and shoving. Prince Charminger was first in line.

One contestant who stood out was Baron Brotwurst. He was a head taller than all the others, and had a long crooked nose and tiny, cruel eyes. None of the villagers liked him because it was well known that he mistreated his servants and ate raw onions for breakfast.

However, he was known to be very strong and athletic.

Some folks thought the winner might be Sweeny Stickyfingers... That wasn't his real last name, but everyone called him that because so many valuable things (like wallets, coins, jewels, etc.) seemed to stick to his fingers. They thought he had a good chance in the races because he'd had so much practice running from the sheriff.

Others bet on Peter Picklepicker. He had spent his entire life laboring in the pickle orchards and was strong as an ox.

Prince Musselbaum, a former suitor of Sierra's older sister, showed up in his bright, shiny armor. He was a handsome fellow and all the young maidens thought he was just *awesome*.

A few folks even bet on Prince Wellred. He wasn't much of an athlete, but he could count up to six hundred and eighty-four and read books three inches thick.

Folks figured anybody that smart might figure out a way to win.

King Albert the Ample, from a nearby kingdom, was so used to getting everything he wanted that he thought for sure he could win a simple thing like an olympics.

He was, however, a tad out of shape.

Another contestant the crowd took note of was all dressed in sinister black armor. Bystanders soon dubbed him, 'the Black Knight.'

"Scary looking, isn't he," said one villager.

"I certainly wouldn't want to argue with that fellow!" said another.

No one ever saw him raise the visor on his helmet — even when he talked, so his voice sounded muffled and strange.

"Maybe he's so ugly he doesn't want to show his face," giggled one old woman. "Or maybe he's wanted by the sheriff and doesn't want to be recognized," said another.

Each night in the taverns the old men gossiped about the one called the Black Knight. Their tales became more and more exaggerated...

"Maybe he's an escaped murderer!" claimed one. "Oh, yes, I'm sure of it!" replied one old grandfather. *The rumors spread.*

very evening a messenger from Aunt Venetia's castle rode up with a letter from Sierra to her parents. They were all pretty much the same:

I will not marry anyone except Prince Charminger. I will drown myself in the moat first!

love, Sierra

PS Aunt Venetia sends her love.

Announcements went out to every town in the kingdom describing the rules to be used in the Pickle-Chiffon Pie Olympics.

By Order of the King

There will be the usual races along with the ogre jump, the discus throw, using Pickle-Chiffon Pies supplied by the castle kitchen, the 100 yard moat swim, dragon wrestling, the giant climb, the horseshoe toss, and the ten-mile bicycle race.

A different event will be held each day, with the winner that day receiving ten points and the others scoring less according to how well they did.

On opening day the king gave a fine speech (although some said a bit too long) and the first event got underway.

It was the horseshoe toss, made more difficult by the fact that the shoes were still attached to the horse.

One by one the contestants took their turns. They grunted and groaned and sweated and strained and tried their very hardest.

Bruno, the blacksmith, had thrown the horseshoes the farthest and was awarded ten points. The unpopular Baron Brotwurst came in second with nine points. Far down the list with only five points each were Prince Charminger and Peter Picklepicker.

That evening the king and queen got another message from Sierra. It was about the same: She would throw herself into the moat if she could not marry Prince Charminger.

They went to bed that night with sad hearts — especially the king, who was beginning to think that the whole idea of the games was a bad one.

"What if Baron Brotwurst wins? Oh dear! I'll only have myself to blame!"

On the second day Baron Brotwurst came in first. It was the day of the ogre jump and he, being an expert horseman, did by far the best by jumping over eight ogres. To everyone's surprise, Peter Picklepicker came in second, followed by Prince Charminger.

On the third day, the day of the 100 yard moat swim,
(four times across) the Black Knight did poorly and
came in a distant last. He had refused to take off his
armor and kept sinking to the bottom.

He made up ground the next day, however, in the giant climb. The one climbing to the top of the giant in the fastest time would win the coveted ten points. Three judges timed the event very carefully.

Somehow the Black Knight had gotten a pair of the king's golf shoes, and with the help of their spikes, had climbed quite swiftly to the top.

The giant complained loudly, but there was no provision in the rules prohibiting the use of golf shoes.

Second that day was Virgil Chadwick, the chimney sweep, who was quite experienced at climbing to high places.

Sweeny Stickyfingers didn't do as well in the races as folks thought he would. He was so used to being chased by the authorities that he kept leaving the track and dashing down dark alleys.

The dragon wrestling didn't fare well, either. Although a crowd pleaser, several contestants were injured and the queen insisted that the event be cancelled.

Peter Picklepicker made a tremendous effort and won the Pickle-Chiffon Pie throwing event. All those years toiling in the pickle orchards had paid off!

On the night before the final day's competition, Prince Charminger, Baron Brotwurst and the Black Knight were all tied for first place. The queen was frantic. "What if that horrid Brotwurst wins tomorrow? Oh, what have we done to our daughter?"

"I don't think that scary Black Knight looks like such good son-in-law material, either!" exclaimed the king. He admitted then that Prince Charminger was their best hope.

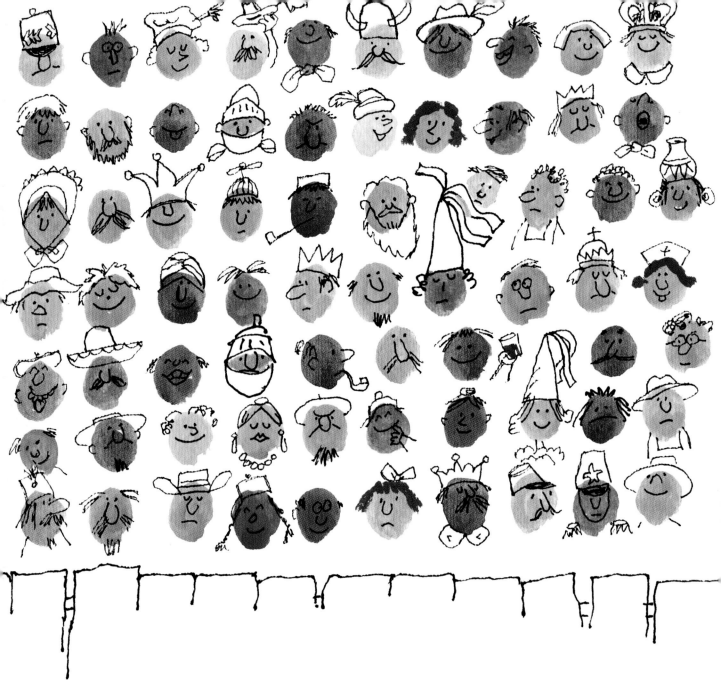

The next day the queen peered up into the stands, hoping to see Sierra. "You'd think she'd want to be here to see what's happening — after all, the winner is to be her husband!

"LOOK!" she cried. "Is that her up there? Is it? Is it? Second row from the top...seventh one over from the left!"

"No," said the king sadly. "Just another pretty girl with red hair."

The last, and deciding, event was the ten-mile bicycle race, made harder by the fact that bicycles hadn't been invented yet so the contestants would have to run. It was a hot day and the pace would be grueling.

All the runners lined up, and since starting pistols hadn't been invented yet, either, the king shot an arrow into the air and yelled, "BANG!"

THEY WERE OFF!

The runners stayed in a tight group for a while, and then Baron Brotwurst started to pull away. His long legs were an advantage.

By the seventh or eighth mile he was well ahead of the others. Prince Charminger and the Black Knight seemed to be weakening, and all the others were far behind.

With only a half mile to go it seemed that the Baron would win easily, but suddenly the Black Knight sped up and soon was right behind him.

Trying to pass him, the Black Knight gave him an accidental bump. Brotwurst stumbled and fell in a heap.

He struggled to get up but it was apparent he had hurt his ankle and would not be able to continue.

Seeing this, Prince Charminger gritted his teeth and grimly tried to close the gap between him and the Black Knight. But the effort was too much for him — with just a few yards to go he stumbled and fell to his knees. He could go no farther.

Then something very strange happened...the Black Knight stopped, came back, and helped Charminger to his feet. Holding him up for the last few yards, the knight pushed him ahead and over the finish line. PRINCE CHARMINGER HAD WON!

The crowd cheered both the prince, for winning, and the Black Knight for being such a good sport.

he king proudly presented a huge trophy to the prince, along with a gift certificate for a lifetime supply of Pickle-Chiffon Pie from the queen.

"You have won the Olympics and the hand of my daughter!" he said. "The queen and I are truly pleased and only wish that Princess Sierra was here to share this joyous moment!"

"Oh, but I *am,* Father!" said a muffled voice from inside the Black Knight's armor.

With that, Princess Sierra pulled off the heavy black armor and flung her arms into the air; her red hair gleaming in the sun and a radiant smile on her face.

The surprised crowd cheered! The king and queen cheered! And Prince Charminger cheered loudest of all!

hat night there was dancing in the streets. Even Baron Brotwurst danced. (It turned out he wasn't such a bad fellow after all.)

Musicians played, bells rang from the church tower and people sang at the top of their voices!

Plans for the royal wedding were made. Aunt Venetia insisted on giving a shower for the bride. The queen baked one hundred and forty-three Pickle-Chiffon Pies for the festivities...and an extra one for the king.

And best of all, Princess Sierra kissed her father and said, "Daddy will you forgive me for being such a stubborn daughter?"

"I will," he smiled, "if you forgive me for being such a stubborn father."

One last thing you should know...

Aunt Venetia, who had been taking organ lessons since she was seven years old, played the huge organ during the wedding ceremony. Although all she knew how to play was, "Twinkle, Twinkle, Little Star," everyone said she did a fine job.